THERE'S A
DRAGON
IN MY SLEEPING BAG

OTHER ATHENEUM BOOKS BY
JAMES HOWE

THERE'S A
DRAGON
IN MY SLEEPING BAG

by James Howe   *illustrated by David S. Rose*

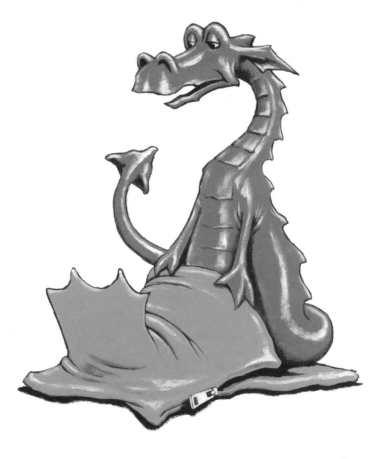

ATHENEUM   1994   NEW YORK

Maxwell Macmillan Canada
Toronto

Maxwell Macmillan International
New York   Oxford   Singapore   Sydney

Atheneum
Macmillan Publishing Company
866 Third Avenue
New York, NY 10022

Maxwell Macmillan Canada, Inc.
1200 Eglinton Avenue East
Suite 200
Don Mills, Ontario M3C 3N1

Macmillan Publishing Company is part of the
Maxwell Communication Group of Companies.

First edition
Printed in the United States of America
10 9 8 7 6 5 4 3 2 1
The text of this book is set in Korinna.
The illustrations are rendered in acrylics.
Printed on recycled paper

Library of Congress Cataloging-in-Publication Data

Howe, James, 1946-
There's a dragon in my sleeping bag / by James Howe : illustrated by David S. Rose. — 1st ed.
p.   cm.
Summary: Alex is intimidated by his older brother Simon's
imaginary dragon, until he is able to create his own friend—a camel
named Calvin.
ISBN 0-689-31873-1
[1. Brothers—Fiction.   2. Imaginary playmates—Fiction.]
I. Rose, David S., 1947-   ill.   II. Title.
PZ7.H83727Tg   1994
[E]—dc20   93-26572

To Zoe
and our friend Calvin
—J.H.

To Apple
—D.S.R.

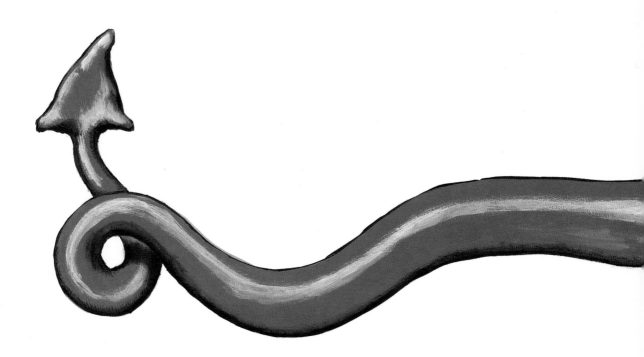

There's a dragon in my sleeping bag. I can't see him, but my brother says he's there.

"You'll have to sleep somewhere else tonight,"
Simon tells me. "If you lie down on top of Dexter,
he'll breathe fire on you and you'll look funny without
any hair."

I sleep on the floor.

At breakfast, there's a dragon in my chair.

"Don't sit there," Simon says, "or Dexter will
breathe fire and burn your bagel."

I hate burned bagels, so I sit in Dad's chair instead.

When I go outside to play, Simon tells me there's a dragon on my swing…

on my end of the seesaw…

and stuck in the middle of the slide.

"I'm going inside," I tell Simon. "It's no fun out here."

But Simon doesn't answer me. He's too busy laughing at something with Dexter.

It used to be just Simon and me. But since this dragon Dexter came to live at our house, Simon doesn't want to play with me anymore.

"I'll play with you."
"Who said that?" I ask.
"My name is Calvin."
"You're a camel."
"It's nice of you to notice," Calvin says. "Want to play?"

I tell Calvin yes, and the best thing
happens. Calvin likes to play the
same games I do. And he always lets
me win.

Not like Simon.

"You can't sleep there," I tell Simon that night.
"Why not?" Simon asks.
"Because there's a camel in your sleeping bag."
Simon can't see Calvin just like I can't see Dexter.
He gives me a dirty look, but he doesn't say
anything.

In the morning, I tell him, "Sorry, Simon, you'll have to sit somewhere else. That's Calvin's seat and if you sit on top of him he'll breathe camel breath on you."

When we go outside to play,

both swings are busy....

There's no room on the seesaw....

And Calvin wants to be the one to help Dexter when he gets stuck in the middle of the slide.

Simon frowns. He mumbles, "Dexter was more fun before Calvin got here."

That night, we have to put two more chairs at the table. "My," Mom says, "if I'd known we were going to have so much company for dinner, I would have roasted a larger chicken."

"That's okay," I tell her. "Calvin is a vegetarian."
Everyone laughs at that.
Everyone but Simon.

When it's time for bed, Calvin and Dexter are already in our sleeping bags. "I'm not sleeping on the floor the way we did last night," Simon says.

"Me either," I say.

So I move Calvin into my room. And Dexter sleeps in Simon's room. And Simon and I don't get to sleep together anymore.

Then one morning…
"Dexter's gone,"
Simon tells me.
"Too bad," I say.
Simon nods. "He
moved to Boston."
"How do you know?"
"Um, he left me a note," Simon tells me.
"Where is it?" I ask.
"Someplace," Simon says. "I forget. You want to
go outside and play?"
"No thanks," I say, "I told Calvin I'd take him for a ride."

"This is supposed to be fun," I tell Calvin. "Why are you so down in the dumps? Don't you like riding with me?"

"Sure," Calvin says. "It's just...well, I miss someone."

"Oh," is all I say, because I have to use the rest of my breath for pedaling up a hill.

"What are you doing?" Simon asks when I drag my sleeping bag into his room that night.

"I'm going to sleep in here with you."

"But what about Calvin?"

"He's gone," I say. "He left a note. See?

"'Dear Alex. I have moved to Boston. I will miss you but I miss Dexter more. That's the way it is with best friends. Goodbye. Calvin.'"

Simon nods. "Well, at least we don't have to worry about camel breath anymore."

"Yep," I say. "Or dragon breath, either."

"Good night, Alex."

"Good night, Simon."

"You know what, Alex? I feel sorry for Dexter and Calvin."

"You do? Why?"

"Because they're only best friends, but we're brothers."

"Yeah," I say. "Hey, Simon."

"What?"

"Will you play with me tomorrow?"

"Of course, Alex. After all, what's a brother for?"